Long ago, when we were little, me and Chrissy did something bad.
We said we were going to Annie's house to play, but we didn't.

We went fishing. All by ourselves.
Which wasn't allowed.
Chrissy said there was a *magic* pond in Bluebell Wood.

The Bog Baby

Written by Jeanne Willis   Illustrated by Gwen Millward

PUFFIN

For my mother, xxx - J.W.
For Mum and Dad, with love - G.M.

PUFFIN BOOKS
Published by the Penguin Group: London, New York, Australia,
Canada, India, Ireland, New Zealand and South Africa
Penguin Books Ltd, Registered Offices: 80 Strand, London WC2R 0RL, England

puffinbooks.com

First published 2008
1 3 5 7 9 10 8 6 4 2
Text copyright © Jeanne Willis, 2008
Illustrations copyright © Gwen Millward, 2008
Printed in China
ISBN: 978-0-141-50030-0

It was only ever there in spring.
   When it rained, it made a huge puddle in the dell
and pond creatures came. We could fish for newts, she said.
                              I won't tell if you won't. So we went.

We found the pond.
It was squelchy
round the edge.
The bluebells squeaked under our boots.

We fished
and
fished,
but we didn't catch a newt.

We caught something much better.

We caught a Bog Baby.

He was the size of a frog, only round and blue.
   He had boggly eyes and a spiky tail
and I do remember he had ears like a mouse.

He came swinging through the flower stalks
and jumped into the water.

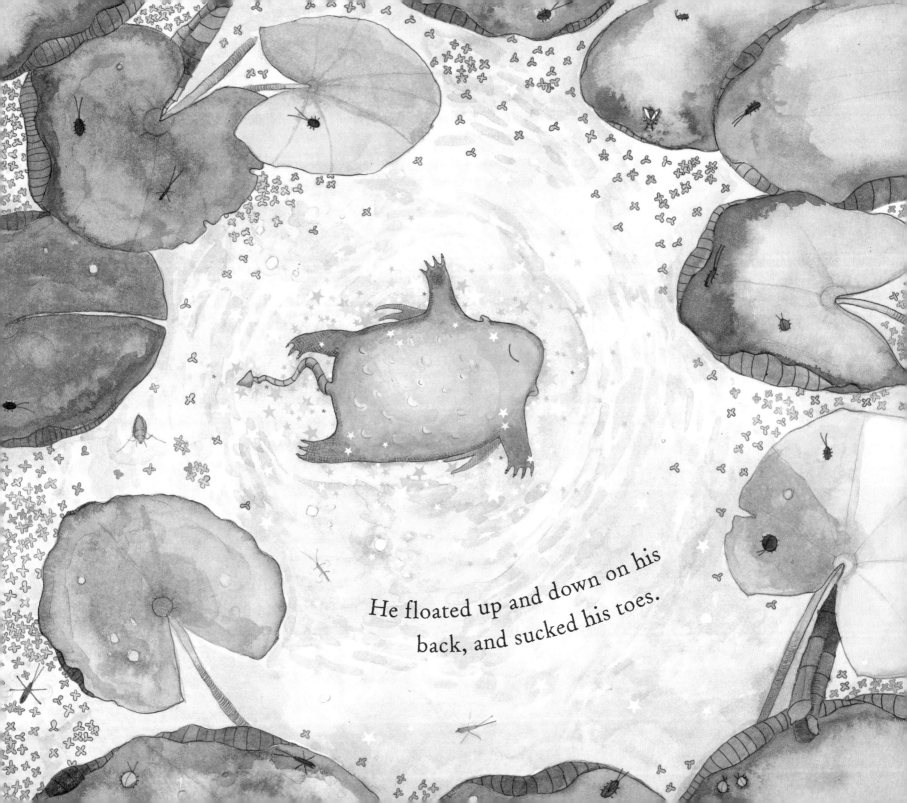

He floated up and down on his
back, and sucked his toes.

That's when I fished him out.

He didn't struggle.

He sat in my hand and
looked surprised.

He was as soft as jelly.

Like he had no bones.

When we stroked him, he flapped his wings.
They were no bigger than daisy petals.
They seemed too small for him to fly.

Chrissy said he might be able to fly
if we *blew* on his wings.

We *blew* and *blew,* but all we did was blow him on to the mud.
He didn't try to escape. He just sat still with his paws over his eyes.

$\mathcal{W}$e put him in a jam jar, took him home and hid him in the shed.

He was **our** Bog Baby.
He wasn't meant to be a secret.
We wanted to show Mum, but we daren't.
If we did, she'd know we didn't go to Annie's.

We made our Bog Baby
a beautiful home in a bucket.

Gravel.

Shells.

Clean water.

Whenever he saw us,
he jumped up and down.
We picked him up and
played with him.

He was very ticklish.
We fed him on cake crumbs.

We **loved** our Bog Baby.

Our friends loved him too. We sneaked him into school in a margarine tub. When the teacher wasn't looking, he played in the sandpit and the water tray.

In the afternoon, he slept in his tub on a piece of damp cotton wool.

Chrissy made him a collar and lead and we took him for
walks in the field. Once, a crow nearly ate him,
but we scared it away just in time.

$\mathcal{W}$e took great care of our Bog Baby.
At least, we tried. But he got sick.

He didn't jump up and down any more.
He went pale and his wings drooped.

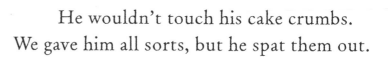

He wouldn't touch his cake crumbs.
We gave him all sorts, but he spat them out.

We wanted to ask Mum for help, but we daren't.
Because of Annie.

But the Bog Baby got thinner.
He wouldn't walk on his lead.
He hid under his shell.

He wouldn't come out, no matter how much we loved him.

Mum found us in the shed.

Chrissy wouldn't say why we were crying.
We'd promised not to tell, but I blabbed.
Mum wasn't angry, though.

When she saw who was in the bucket, she smiled and her eyes went misty.
She said she hadn't seen a Bog Baby since she was little.

Please make him better, we cried.
We love him **so much**.

I know, she said.
But the Bog Baby is a wild thing.
He doesn't belong here.
He isn't meant to eat cake.
Or walk on a lead.
Or sleep in a tub.

She picked up
the bucket and we
followed her out.

If we really loved
the Bog Baby, we had to
do what was best for him.
No matter how much it hurt us.

That was **real love**.
That's why we let him go.

ʙack where he belonged.

Living in the wood.
Playing in the pond.
Sleeping in the damp leaves under the moon.

*W*e never saw him again.
I think he grew up and had babies of his own.

Last spring, my daughter found the
*magic pond and guess what she saw . . .

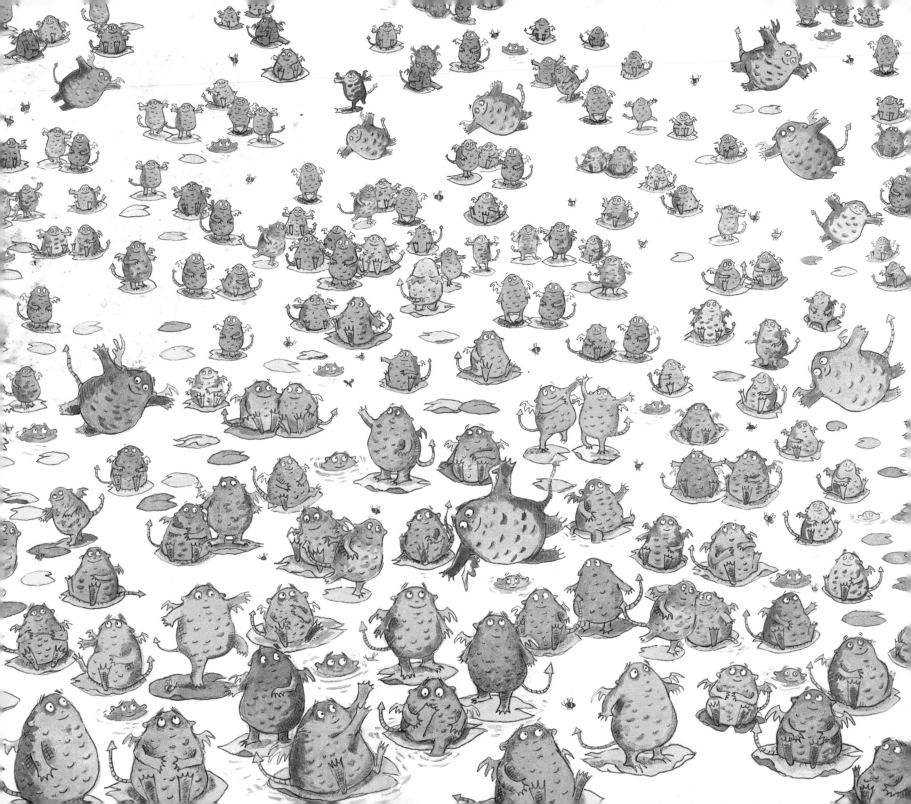

Hundreds of Bog Babies swinging through the bluebells.

Catching flies.

Floating on their backs.

Sucking their toes.

That's what she told me.
And that's what I believe.

Notes about your Bog Baby

When you find your very own Bog Baby, you can write all about him here.

Where did you find him? . . . .

What is his favourite food? . . . .

How many toes does he have? . . . .

What is his favourite flower? . . . .

Does he croak, purr or tweet? . . . .

Bog Babies are extremely rare. Very little is known about them. If you are lucky enough to find one,
it would be helpful if you could make notes and a small sketch and send them to S.O.B.B. (Save Our Bog Babies)
at the following address: Puffin Picture Books, 80 Strand, London WC2R 0RL.